AKBAR AND BIRBAL STORIES

Contents

How Akbar and Birbal Met

Emperor Akbar was very fond of hunting.
As a little boy, he would leave his lessons
and go riding and hunting. He grew up to
be a better rider and a more fearless hunter
than any of his courtiers.

One day, while chasing a tiger, Akbar
and a few of his brave soldiers got lost. By
sunset, they were far away from the royal
capital of Agra. They were very tired and
exhausted. They reached a place where
three roads met.

"Which road should we take to go back to Agra?" wondered the emperor aloud. "Which road do you think leads to Agra?"

All three roads looked the same to him. The emperor's men were confused too. Just then, a young man came walking down one of the roads.

The emperor's men were very relieved to see the young man. They asked him to come forward. He did so, while looking curiously at the well-dressed royal visitors who stood before him.

Then Emperor Akbar asked him, "Young man, do you know which one of these roads goes to Agra?"

The young man smiled and said, "Sir, everybody knows that roads do not go to Agra or anywhere else."

He started laughing at his own joke. "It is people who go from one place to another," said the young man.

The emperor's men thought, 'How can this young man joke with the king?'

"No, they don't," said the emperor laughing. His soldiers also joined him.

"What is your name?" Akbar asked the man.

"Mahesh Das," he replied.

The emperor took off a huge emerald ring from his finger and gave it to the man. "You are speaking to Akbar, the emperor of Hindustan," he said.

9

"We need brave young men like you in our court. Bring this ring with you whenever you come to our capital, and I shall recognise you immediately. Now, show us the road we must take in order to reach Agra," said the emperor.

Mahesh Das bowed before the king and pointed towards one of the roads. Then the emperor and his men galloped away into the distance, while Mahesh Das looked on till he could no longer see them.

Mahesh Das and the Sentry

When Mahesh Das finished his studies, he decided to go to Agra and meet the emperor. On reaching Agra, he was dazzled by its huge *havelis* and the bustling *bazaar*. These sights were new to him, as he had spent his entire life in a poor village.

Mahesh Das had the king's emerald ring with him. It was nearly evening when he arrived at the king's fort.

It was a massive and grand fort located on the banks of the River Yamuna. The fort was guarded by fierce-looking sentries with spears in their hands.

Mahesh Das went up to one of the soldiers and told him that he had been invited by the emperor.

The soldier looked at the dusty villager in front of him and said mockingly, "The emperor of Hindustan would like to meet *you*!"

"Maybe," said Mahesh Das boldly, though he felt quite scared. "Here, I have the emperor's ring to prove it," he added, taking out the ring which the emperor had given him.

The guard looked at him doubtfully.

"That is no ordinary ring," said a pundit, who had stopped to watch, "you should let this man go in."

The guard agreed but only if Mahesh Das promised to share the gift that the emperor would give him.

Mahesh Das agreed at once and the guard let him in.

The emperor was in the *Diwan-i-Aam* (the Hall of Public Audience).

The palace was grand with rich carpets on the floor and intricately carved patterns on the walls. The emperor sat on a platform at the far end of the hall.

Bowing low, Mahesh Das carefully made his way towards the throne. The courtiers in the hall wondered who he was.

The emperor immediately recognised him. He asked him to come forward and make a wish.

"Your Majesty, I just want to be given fifty lashes," he requested.

"Is he a madman?" the courtiers whispered among themselves.

But the emperor liked his straightforward manner and asked him the reason behind the request.

"Your Majesty," replied Mahesh Das, "the sentry at the gate allowed me into the fort only if I agreed to one condition – that I give him half of the gift that I receive from you. I am ready to bear twenty-five lashes in order to share it with the guard."

Akbar was enraged when he heard this. "Bring this greedy guard to me who keeps my subjects away from me!" he thundered. The guard was immediately brought before the king.

The king sentenced the guard to the entire fifty lashes. Never again did the sentry try to bully poor people who came to meet the emperor.

The emperor was impressed with the quick wit and intelligence of Mahesh Das. He decided to give him a place in his court. He also conferred the title of 'Raja Birbal' on him. This is how Birbal became a part of Akbar's court.

King Akbar's
Mahabharata

Once, Birbal brought the Mahabharata for Akbar. A few days later, Akbar said, "You must write an Akbari Mahabharata, Birbal."

Birbal wondered, 'A great sage wrote the Mahabharata. How can I equal this feat?'

He thought for a while and said, "Your Majesty, I need two months and fifty thousand gold coins."

Akbar agreed to give him the money. With some of it he bought some papers and donated the rest of the money to the brahmins.

After two months, Akbar asked, "Is the book ready yet, Birbal?"

"Almost," said Birbal, "Ten brahmins are helping me in the task. I need some more money to ask five more." Akbar agreed.

Having bound up all the papers, Birbal returned to the court in a month. "The book is ready. But first, I must see the queen," he pleaded.

So he went to the queen, who was delighted to see the book.

Then Birbal said, "Your Highness, according to this story, you should also have five husbands like Draupadi and must suffer the same fate as she did."

The queen was angry. "What rubbish! Burn that book now!" she ordered. Birbal slipped out to inform King Akbar.

The king was shocked when he heard about it. Then, Birbal said, "Your Majesty, every age has a new story to tell."

The king understood and praised Birbal.

The Stolen Bottle

Once, King Akbar went to his wives. He said, "Each of you is to tell me a silly tale. The one who tells the silliest tale will be rewarded."

When Birbal overheard him, he thought, 'Something is not right. The king doesn't make such silly demands.'

Birbal decided not to visit the court. So, Akbar went to meet him but Birbal had gone outside. His daughter received the king.

Meanwhile, Birbal went to the king's room in the palace. There, he saw many wine bottles lying in the cupboard! Birbal understood the reason behind the king's silly behaviour. Birbal picked up a bottle of wine and left.

On the way, he met Akbar. "Birbal, where have you been?" asked Akbar, "And what are you hiding in the shawl?"

Birbal replied that it was nothing. "It's a parrot!" he said. "It's a horse... No, it's an elephant... Actually, it's a donkey," Birbal muttered. Akbar got angry. Then, Birbal took the wine bottle out.

They went to the palace. There, Akbar saw a bottle missing from his cupboard. He knew that Birbal had taken it. He asked Birbal about it.

"Sire, when I said I had nothing, I meant that wine affects our senses," said Birbal, explaining his riddle. "When I said 'parrot', I meant that one behaves like a parrot. At the third cup, one acts like a horse. At the fourth cup, like an elephant, and like a foolish donkey at the fifth cup."

Akbar realised his foolishness and threw away all the wine bottles.

The Queen's Victory

Once, Akbar was chatting with his queen. He remarked, "Birbal is the most prized jewel of my court. He is unchallenged in wit and intelligence."

The queen laughed and said, "In wit, I can defeat Birbal any day." So Akbar asked her to prove it.

Birbal was summoned. The queen called the maid and asked for sherbat and sweets to be brought in. Then she counted till ten, and said, "Now, the sherbat and the sweets are ready. Here they come."

Just as she said this, the maid entered with the dishes. The queen said to Birbal, "Did you notice that just as I finished counting, the refrshments arrived? We will come to your house for lunch tomorrow."

Birbal bowed and left. Akbar asked her why she had not proved herself.

"Wait for tomorrow, sire," she said, smiling.

The next day, at Birbal's house, the queen said, "Surely, lunch is ready, Birbal. Now count and tell me exactly when the dishes will come, just as I did yesterday."

Smiling, Birbal said, "Your Majesty, I ask you to count and lunch will arrive."

The queen agreed. When she stopped counting, the servants entered with the dishes, just as they had been told by Birbal.

The queen admitted Birbal's victory. But Birbal said to the queen, "You have won, your Highness, for the lunch arrived when you stopped counting!"

"How clever, Birbal!" said the queen, "You made me win even when I lost."

Akbar had a hearty laugh.

What I Desire

Once, there lived a foolish miser. He kept all his money hidden in a large box in a corner of his home.

One day, a fire broke out in his house. As the fire grew in strength, he cried out louder. His neighbours rushed towards his home, carrying buckets of water. "All my wealth lies there in a box," he wept.

A greedy goldsmith overheard him and said, "I'll go and get the box for you, but only on one condition. After I get the box, I'll give you only what I desire. The rest is mine."

The desperate miser hastily agreed to the goldsmith's conditions. The goldsmith jumped into the flames. Soon he returned with the box.

The goldsmith said, "You promised me that I could give you what I desire. Here, take the box. The gems and coins are all mine."

"That's unfair. You can keep half my savings but I will take the other half," said the miser. But the goldsmith would not listen. They argued for some time.

Then the miser and the goldsmith decided to go to Birbal for justice. Birbal thought for a while and said, "Goldsmith, you promised the miser what you desire. What do *you* desire?" asked Birbal, carefully.

"The gems and the coins," replied the goldsmith immediately.

"Then, these are the miser's as you promised to give him what you desire," said Birbal. Realising that he had been tricked, the goldsmith returned everything to the miser.

The Washerman and the Potter

Once, a washerman's donkey entered the potter's yard and broke all the pots. The potter beat the poor donkey badly. The washerman rushed to its rescue. He paid for the broken pots but the potter was still angry.

He went to King Akbar and said, "Your Majesty, the Shah of Iran says his elephants are white and clean, while ours are black and dirty. Sir, the Shah's washermen clean his elephants daily."

Akbar declared, "All the washermen in Agra must wash our elephants."

"Sir, my neighbour washes very well. He can scrub all our elephants," he said.

So the washerman was called forth. He scrubbed all day long but the elephants still remained black. He realised the potter's trick and went to seek Birbal's help.

The next day, Akbar scolded the washerman, but he said, "Sire, I need a huge pot to dip the elephants while cleaning them."

Akbar asked the potter to build a large pot. However, when the elephant stepped into it, it broke. Angered, Akbar ordered for another pot. The potter knew he had been outwitted and begged pardon.

Then, Akbar asked the washerman, "Who gave you this idea to outsmart the potter?"

"Sire, it was Birbal," he said. Akbar was very pleased with Birbal.

Birbal in Burma

Hussain Khan, Akbar's brother-in-law wished to be the minister in Birbal's place. He tried all means to influence the court.

One courtier said to Akbar, "We have had a Hindu as minister for far too long. Give the post to a Muslim now. Hussain Khan would be the ideal choice."

Akbar was angry as he believed that all religions were equal, but he replied, "I want Hussain Khan to accompany Birbal to deliver this letter to the king of Burma."

When Birbal and Khan reached Burma, Birbal gave the letter to the king of Burma, who became worried after reading it. The two visitors were then taken to the guest palace but kept under heavy security. Birbal and Hussain Khan wondered why so many guards were stationed around them.

Later, the Burmese minister told them, "Your king has ordered that both of you are to be killed on the full moon night."

"Please carry out our king's instructions," Birbal merely said.

"Yes," Hussain Khan rejoined.

The minister immediately went to the king of Burma and told him about Birbal and Hussain Khan's behaviour.

Meanwhile, Birbal said to Hussain Khan, "Listen carefully, if you wish to be saved, do as I say. When we are taken to be hanged, insist on being hanged before me. I will handle the rest myself. Do as I say or else, we both will die."

Three days later, on the full moon night, they were taken to be hanged. Birbal told the king, "Your Majesty, please hang me first."

Then Hussain Khan said, "No, I should be hanged first as I am Akbar's relative."

The king of Burma was puzzled. He asked Birbal, "Why do you want to be hanged first?"

"Your Majesty, it is believed that the one who is hanged first tonight will be born as the king of Burma in his next birth," said Birbal.

The king thought, 'I want my own son to be the next king of Burma.' So he released them and sent them back to Emperor Akbar.

When they returned, Akbar asked Hussain Khan, "Do you want to take up Birbal's post now?"

"Sire, I am not ready yet," he said, "Birbal is better suited than I am." Thus, Birbal won over another of his enemies.

A Matter of Crows

The king's palace had the *Diwan-i-Aam* and a beautiful *Diwan-i-Khas*. The *Diwan-i-Khas* was smaller than the *Diwan-i-Aam* but lavishly furnished. All the courtiers met here to discuss important matters and issues.

Sometimes, the king asked strange questions which Birbal alone could answer.

Once, Akbar asked his courtiers to find out how many crows there were in Agra. He warned them to carefully check before answering.

The courtiers were scared. Nobody knew the number of crows in the city!

The courtiers were in a fix. If they did not answer, they would be punished, and if they were wrong, then too, they would be punished. Some courtiers began to pray, while some looked at the sky trying to count the crows.

Only Birbal was calm. He said, "Your Majesty, there are exactly ten thousand, six hundred and sixty-six crows in Agra."

"Are you sure, Birbal?" asked the emperor, "We shall have the crows counted to make sure that this number is correct."

"By all means, Your Majesty," said Birbal, calmly. "But I cannot be sure that all the crows will remain in Agra till the counting is over. Many may visit their friends and relatives in Delhi. Then there will be less crows than the number I gave you.

"Also, many relatives and friends of these crows may visit them in Agra, so it might increase the number. But I can surely say that at this moment, there are exactly ten thousand, six hundred and sixty-six crows in Agra."

The king burst out laughing and said, "Birbal, you are amazing!"

Length of the Stick

Once, there lived a very rich merchant in Agra. One day, a burglary took place in his house. The merchant suspected one of his numerous servants but he did not know who the thief was. So he went to Birbal and asked for his help.

Birbal heard the merchant's problem and went to his house. There, Birbal called all the servants and spoke to them, "You all know about the burglary that took place here. If any one of you has committed the crime, come forward and admit it now. You will be forgiven."

But nobody came forward. Then Birbal came up with a clever plan. He gave each servant a stick and asked him to keep it carefully. He said to them, "The sticks given to you are of equal length. They have magical powers. The stick kept by the thief will grow two inches longer by tomorrow."

51

Now the servant who had committed the theft, was very worried. He could not sleep well that night. He knew that he would get caught as his stick would grow two inches longer than before. Then an idea struck him. He got up and cut his stick two inches short, thinking that if the stick grew, it would remain the same length as those of the others. With a sigh of relief, he went off to sleep.

Next morning, Birbal returned to the merchant's house. He called all the servants and asked them to bring their sticks with them. The servants obeyed him.

After glancing at their sticks, he pulled out the culprit and said to the merchant, "Here is your thief."

The servant fell at Birbal's feet and begged for his forgiveness. The merchant thanked Birbal and asked him if the stick was really magical and had grown two inches longer.

Birbal laughed and said, "Oh, those were just ordinary sticks. But the thief was scared that his stick would grow longer, so he cut it and his stick became shorter than the rest. So I looked for the man with the shorter stick."

Thus, Birbal helped to catch the thief. The merchant and the servants praised Birbal's intelligence.

Half-Light, Half-Shadow

Once Akbar, in a fit of anger, asked Birbal to leave the city. Birbal agreed, but before leaving, he said that he would enter the city only when the emperor asked him to return.

Many days passed and Akbar started missing his friend. He wanted Birbal to come back. So he sent his men in search of Birbal. They looked for him everywhere, but could not find him.

Then the king had an idea. He announced a reward of a thousand gold coins for any man who would come to the court in half-light and half-shadow. The king knew that Birbal would not be able to resist this challenge.

Now Birbal was staying with a brahmin in a small village. He heard of the king's proclamation.

He wanted to repay the brahmin for his kindness. He asked the brahmin if he had heard of the king's proclamation.

"Yes, I have. But how is it possible to go in half-light and half-shadow?" asked the brahmin.

Birbal asked the brahmin to follow his instructions.

He said to the brahmin, "Go to the palace carrying a *charpoy* (cot) on your head. Thus, you will be half in light and half in shadow."

So the brahmin went to the palace carrying the *charpoy* on his head.

The king was very happy and said, "Brahmin, before I give you your reward, tell me if this was really your idea or somebody else's."

The brahmin was scared and spoke the truth. He said, "A poor brahmin, who has been staying with me for the past few weeks, gave me this idea."

The king knew that this brahmin could be none other than Birbal himself. He gave the brahmin his reward and sent his men to the brahmin's house to bring Birbal back. Birbal promptly returned to the palace. The king was very glad to have Birbal back again.

Who is the Greater Fool?

Once, King Akbar asked Birbal to make a list of all the fools in the city of Agra. So Birbal set out to complete the task. He searched the streets looking for fools and wrote down their names on his list.

Meanwhile, a merchant from a faraway land arrived at Akbar's court. He had brought a horse with him. The king asked the merchant about the purpose of his visit to his city.

"Your Majesty, I sell horses of the finest breed. I have brought this horse as a sample. Please take a look," said the merchant.

Now Akbar was very fond of horses. He had numerous horses already, but he could not resist the offer and went with the merchant to see the horse. "This is a really fine horse," said Akbar.

"Your Majesty, I have more than a hundred such horses. Would you like to buy them all, your Majesty?" asked the merchant.

"Yes, I would like to buy all the horses! When can you bring them?" asked the king.

"Your Majesty, I would have brought them, but the transportation of so many horses requires a lot of money, and I didn't have so much money. If you would be kind enough to give me one lakh gold coins, then I will bring them all in a fortnight," said the merchant.

The king ordered his treasurer to give the merchant one lakh gold coins. After taking them, the merchant left, promising to return as soon as possible with the horses.

Akbar was very happy with himself, thinking that he had struck a good bargain. He showed Birbal the horse which he had bought from the merchant. He also told Birbal that he had given the merchant one lakh gold coins in advance, so that he could bring the rest of the horses.

"You mean you have given the merchant so much money in advance?" said Birbal, disbelievingly.

"Yes, the horses were quite cheap even at that price. So I decided to buy the rest of the horses too," said Akbar.

"But your Majesty, do you have his address, or did someone at the court stand guarantee for him?" asked Birbal.

"No, but he seemed honest. I am sure he will come back. Now have you completed the list of fools?" asked Akbar.

"It is almost finished. I just have to add one more name to it," said Birbal. He quickly wrote down a name and gave it to Akbar.

When Akbar saw the list, he was shocked.

"How dare you write my name on the list?" he thundered. Standing up, he shouted, "You are calling the emperor of Hindustan a fool!"

"I beg your pardon, Your Majesty. But you have just given one lakh gold coins to a complete stranger. Isn't that a very foolish thing to do?" replied Birbal calmly.

Akbar sat down and thought for a minute.

"But what if the merchant returns with the horses after a fortnight?" asked Akbar.

"Then, I will strike off your name from the list and write his name instead," said Birbal. Akbar could not help laughing at this remark. As usual, Birbal got away with a witty answer.

The Most Beautiful Child

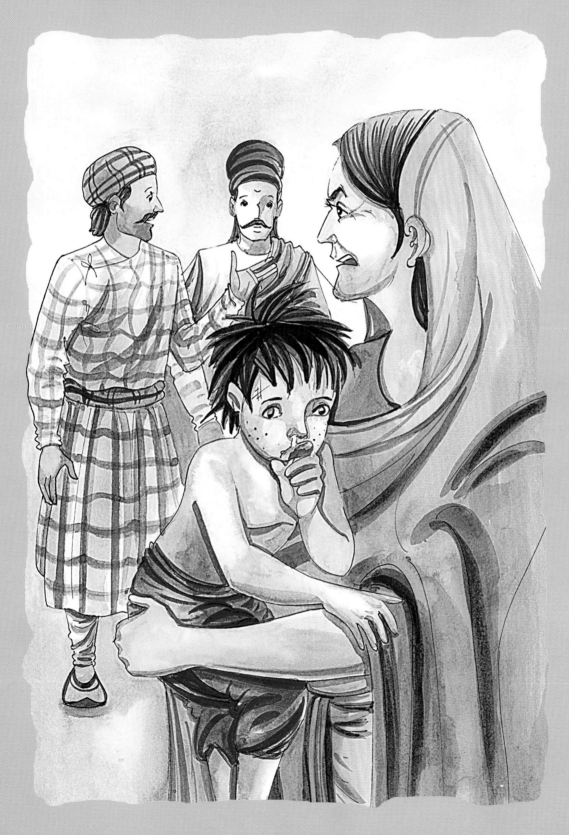

King Akbar adored his grandson and would spend hours playing with him. Even in the court, he would only talk about his grandson.

"There is no child as handsome as my grandson," said Akbar and all the courtiers agreed with him. They dared not refute the claims of the king.

But Birbal said, "Your Majesty, the young prince is very good-looking indeed, but all parents find their children beautiful."

This angered Akbar. So, one of his courtiers suggested that each of them bring a child whom he thought to be the most beautiful. Then, they could judge who was the most beautiful child.

The next day, each courtier brought a child with him. The king saw them all, but he insisted that his grandson was the most handsome child. Finally, he came to Birbal who had been silently standing and watching the scene all the while.

Birbal did not have any child with him. Akbar asked him why he had disobeyed.

Birbal said that although he had seen the most beautiful child in the country, the child's mother did not let him bring it.

"She did not want strangers to cast their eyes on her child," added Birbal.

"Then, we will go in disguise and see the child ourselves," said Akbar.

So Akbar and Birbal, accompanied by a few ministers, travelled to the other end of the city. Birbal took them to a small and dirty hut. A child was playing in the mud. His body was covered with dust and grime. Akbar and his ministers were shocked when they saw the child.

He was the ugliest child they had ever seen. The child had pox marks all over his face. He was dirty and had a running nose.

"Birbal, you call this child beautiful? This is the ugliest child I have ever seen!" said Akbar.

The child's mother overheard him and got very angry.

"How dare you call my child ugly! He is the most beautiful child God has given me. Go away from here at once!" she screamed, and picked up her baby. She wiped his face with a cloth, and hugged and kissed him lovingly. She took her child inside and then closed the door.

There was a shocked silence as the king and his ministers realised what Birbal had tried to show them.

Finally, Akbar turned to Birbal and said, "You were right. All parents find their children to be the most beautiful. The love for their children blinds them, so, they do not see anything wrong with them."

"Your Majesty, the same holds true for grandparents too. Don't you think so?" teased Birbal.

The Punishment

Everybody knew that Akbar was very fond of his grandson and that he loved to spend time with him. One morning, when Akbar was getting ready for the court, his grandson came running to him.

"Grandfather, there is something in your moustache. Bend down and I will take it out," said his grandson.

When Akbar bent down, his grandson pulled out a hair from his moustache!

"Ouch!" screamed Akbar, clutching his face, "Why did you do such a naughty thing?"

"Ha! Ha! I fooled you!" said his grandson. Akbar got up and sent him off to play.

On his way to the court, Akbar thought that he would give his ministers a problem to solve.

When he reached the court, he addressed his courtiers saying, "Someone pulled out a hair from my moustache this morning. I want him to be punished. What punishment should I give him?"

The courtiers were shocked when they heard this. 'How could anybody dare to pull out a hair from the emperor's moustache?' they thought. The courtiers started giving their suggestions.

"The man should be flogged a thousand times," said one courtier.

"He should be imprisoned for life," said another.

"He should be hanged," said a third.

While everybody was giving Akbar suggestions, Birbal kept quiet.

Akbar noticed this. He asked Birbal, "Why are you so quiet? Everyone is giving me plenty of advice but you have not said a word. Don't you have anything to say about this, Birbal?"

81

Birbal told him that he would rather speak in private but the king insisted that he spoke up.

Birbal shocked everybody by saying, "The guilty person should be kissed." He explained that only a child could do such mischief, which could only be his grandson.

He received a lot of praise for his clever deduction.

Those Who Cannot See

Once, while looking at a list of all the blind people in the city, Akbar said, "I see very few names on the list."

Birbal said, "Your Majesty, what about those who don't see even though they have eyes?"

Akbar thought Birbal was joking. So, Birbal asked for a few days to prove his point.

The next day, Birbal went to the marketplace and started weaving a cot.

Everyone was curious to know what Birbal was doing, so they asked him. Birbal did not reply and simply wrote down their names. As the word spread around, more people came to see Birbal and asked him the same question. Birbal remained silent and asked his attendant to write down their names.

Soon the news reached Akbar's ears. Even he was curious to know what Birbal was doing. So he went to the marketplace and saw Birbal weaving a cot. He also asked Birbal what he was doing.

Ignoring the emperor, Birbal said, "That will be two hundred and fifty."

"Birbal, answer me! What are you doing?" asked Akbar, angrily.

"Your Majesty, I am weaving a cot and also making a list of all the blind people," said Birbal, "Today two hundred and fifty people asked me what I was doing, even though I was weaving a cot in broad daylight."

Akbar asked Birbal to show him the list. When he saw the list, he was surprised to see his name on it.

"But why do you have my name here?" asked Akbar, angrily.

"Because you also asked me what I was doing," said Birbal. Thus, Birbal, as usual, had the last word.

Begum and Birbal

Birbal was the king's favourite. Many courtiers were jealous of him.

Once, they decided to have Birbal removed from the minister's post and asked Hussain Khan, the king's brother-in-law, to take Birbal's place.

"But the emperor will never agree while Birbal is here," said Hussain Khan.

"Ask your sister to plead your case with the emperor," said one courtier.

"That's a good idea," said Hussain Khan. Next day, he persuaded his sister to talk to the emperor about it.

When the emperor came, the begum requested him to make her brother the minister in place of Birbal.

This surprised the king who had not expected such a request. He needed somebody intelligent and capable to help him run the vast empire and Birbal was the man best suited for the job.

Also, he needed a valid reason for removing Birbal.

"Give him a tough task to do and when he fails, you can remove him," suggested the begum.

"In that case, you can suggest a task yourself," said the emperor.

"When you are taking a stroll in the garden, ask him to fetch me. I will make sure that he does not succeed," she said.

The king agreed to the queen's request. The next day, while he was taking a stroll, the king sent for Birbal.

Akbar told him to get the queen. "If you fail, you shall be removed from the post of minister," added Akbar.

Birbal realised that his enemies were behind this well thought out plan. To save himself, he came up with another plan and took the help of a messenger.

He went to the queen's palace to escort her to the king, who was in the garden. At the same moment, the messenger arrived with a private message for him.

Birbal excused himself and walked aside to hear the message.

Meanwhile, the begum was curious to listen to the message. So she tried to overhear what they were saying, but the only words she could hear were, "She is beautiful".

Birbal then went back to the begum and said, "The situation has changed. You need not come, begum."

Then Birbal left. But the begum became very suspicious. She hurried to the palace garden only to find the king alone.

Akbar was surprised to see her there despite her promise. She repeated Birbal's words.

"Just because Birbal said the situation had changed, you came running here?" said Akbar, amused.

'How can I tell you that it was the fear of a beautiful maiden with you that brought me here,' thought the begum.

Just then Birbal came, and Akbar said, "Birbal, as usual, you have won!"